READING

Farm Animals

by Deri Robins

Aladdin/Watts
London • Sydney

Contents

AROUND THE FARMYARD   PAGE 4
Farm • Piglets • Pig • Hens • Cockerel
Chick • Turkey • Ducks • Kids • Lamb

IN THE FIELDS   PAGE 14
Cows • Milking • Cattle • Bull • Sheep • Goats

ANIMAL HELPERS   PAGE 22
Shepherd • Sheepdog • Horses • Pulling a plough
Buffalo • Llama

Can You Find? • Do You Know? • Index

© Aladdin Books Ltd 2000

Designed and produced by
Aladdin Books Ltd
28 Percy Street
London W1T 2BZ

First published in
Great Britain in 2000 by
Franklin Watts
96 Leonard Street
London EC2A 4XD

ISBN 0 7496 4849 X

A catalogue record for this book is
available from the British Library.

Printed in the U.A.E.

All rights reserved

Editor
Jim Pipe

Literacy Consultant
Ann Hawken
Oxford Brookes University
Westminster Institute of Education

Design
Flick Book Design and Graphics

Picture Research
Brian Hunter Smart

Meet the animals on a farm. There are pigs, chickens and ducks around the farmyard. Visit cows, sheep and goats out in the fields.

Then find out how dogs and horses help the farmer.

Farmyard

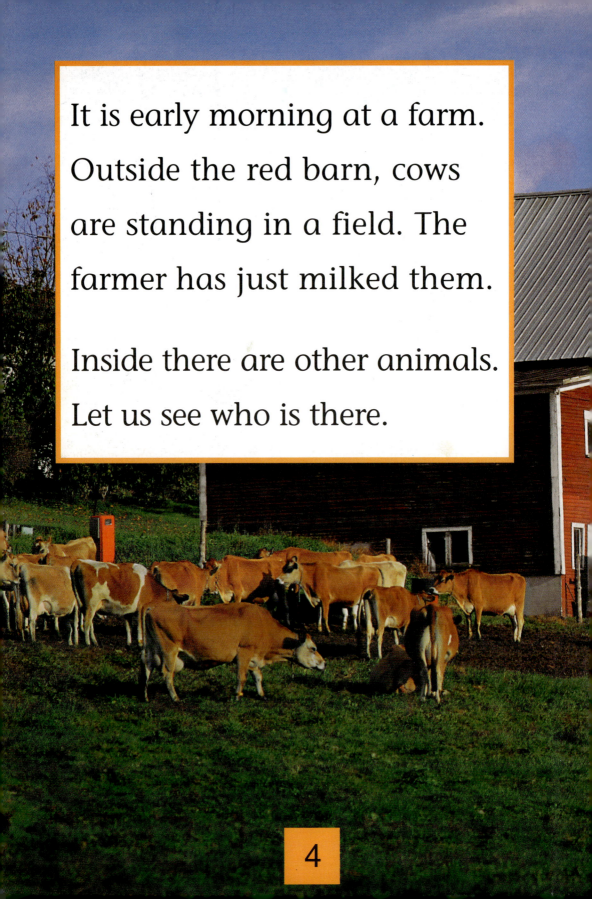

It is early morning at a farm. Outside the red barn, cows are standing in a field. The farmer has just milked them.

Inside there are other animals. Let us see who is there.

Farm
What animals are inside?

AROUND THE FARMYARD

It is feeding time in the pig pen. The little piglets get all the food they need from their mum.

Piglets

AROUND THE FARMYARD

Pigs eat all kinds of food. Some of them dig for food under the ground with their noses.

Pigs love to keep cool in a muddy pool!

Pig

7

AROUND THE FARMYARD

In the hen house, hens scratch for seeds or worms in the ground.

Hens

Cockerel

Outside, a cockerel wakes everyone up with his loud crow, "Cock-a-doodle-doo"!

AROUND THE FARMYARD

Hens lay eggs, and sit on them for a few weeks. When it is time for the chicks to hatch, they break out of the eggs with their beaks.

Chick

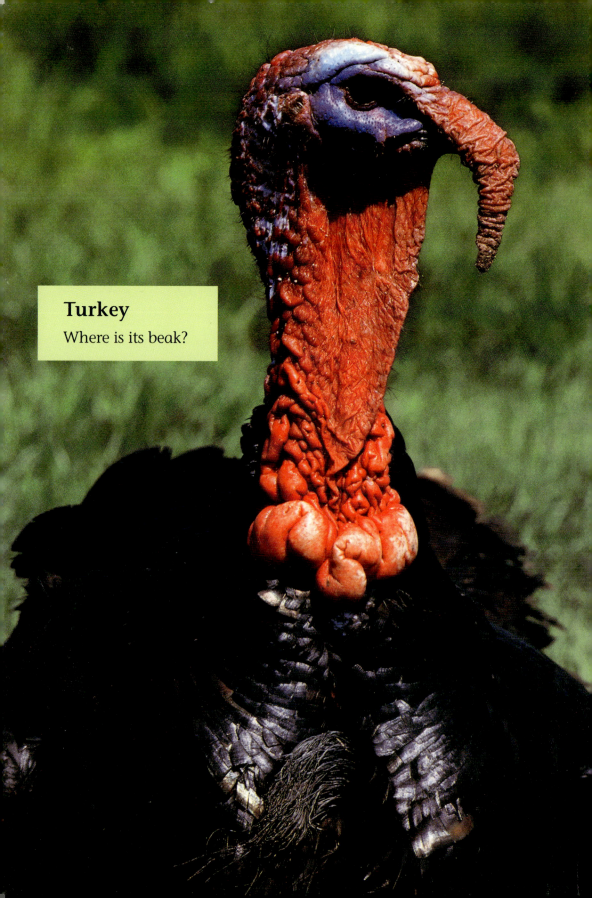

Turkey

Where is its beak?

AROUND THE FARMYARD

Turkeys live in a pen close to the farm. They are bigger than hens and ducks. Most turkeys have a flap of red skin under their beak.

Ducks waddle around the farmyard. Their webbed feet are made for swimming in the pond.

Ducks

AROUND THE FARMYARD

Kids

The farmer often keeps baby animals in the farmyard.

Baby goats like to drink milk. It is like feeding a big, hungry baby!

AROUND THE FARMYARD

Baby goats are called kids, baby sheep are called lambs, and baby cows are called calves.

Lambs drink their mother's milk. When they get older they eat grass.

Lamb

Cows
What are they eating?

IN THE FIELDS

These cows are milked very early in the morning, while you are still asleep in bed. They are milked again in the evening, too.

Milking

The farmer uses a machine to suck the milk from the cows.

IN THE FIELDS

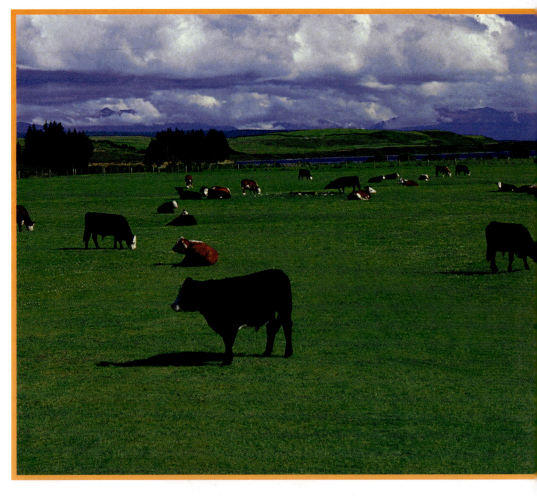

Cattle

Would you like to live on a ranch? A ranch is a big farm where many cattle live.

A group of cattle is called a herd.

IN THE FIELDS

Do you know that cows are cattle mums and bulls are cattle dads?

Bull

If you are a sheep, your soft coat keeps you warm in winter.

This coat is called a fleece. The farmer cuts it off to make wool! But this does not hurt the sheep.

Sheep

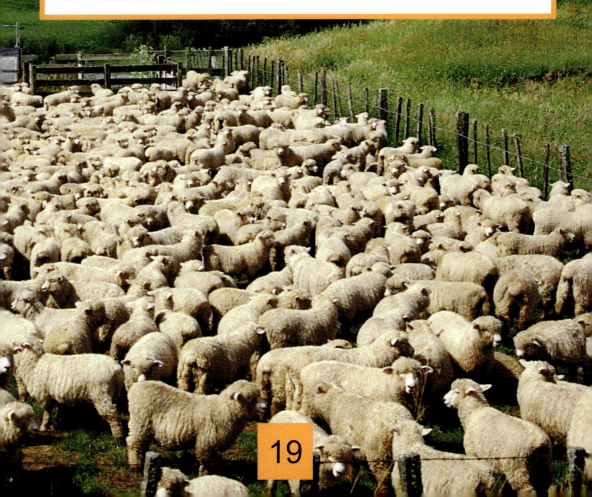

IN THE FIELDS

Sheep and goats often live up in the hills, where the grass is too short for cows.
They live in groups called flocks.

Goats are nimble, quick and tough. They are good at climbing and jumping, too!

Goats

IN THE FIELDS

Some goats live on the steep sides of mountains.

ANIMAL HELPERS

A farmer who looks after sheep is called a shepherd. This shepherd has a friend to help him – a dog!

Shepherd

22

ANIMAL HELPERS

Sheepdog

A dog is quick and nimble. It helps the farmer move the sheep from field to field.

The shepherd whistles to the dog to tell it what to do.

ANIMAL HELPERS

Horses are strong, fast and graceful. Would you like to be a young horse running through the fields?

Horses

ANIMAL HELPERS

On big farms, farmers ride on horses to round up cattle and sheep. Some farmers keep horses just to ride for fun.

ANIMAL HELPERS

Pulling a plough

Not all farms are the same.

In some places farmers use horses, cattle or buffaloes to pull ploughs and heavy carts.

Buffalo

ANIMAL HELPERS

Llama

Some farmers keep strange animals. This llama from South America has a woolly coat like a sheep. It spits when it gets angry!

Can You Find?

Farm animals don't look like us. They have horns and beaks and tails. Can you find the farm animals that have these parts?

Beak

Hoof

Snout

Foot

Tail

The answers are on page 32.

Horns

Clue: Look at pages 7, 9, 12, 17 and 25.

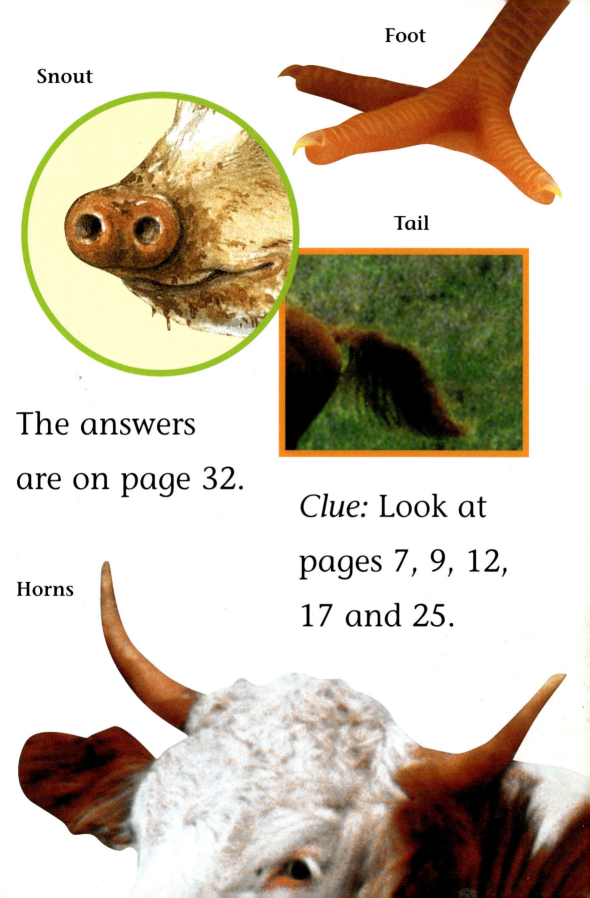

Do You Know?

Do you know what things we get from each animal?

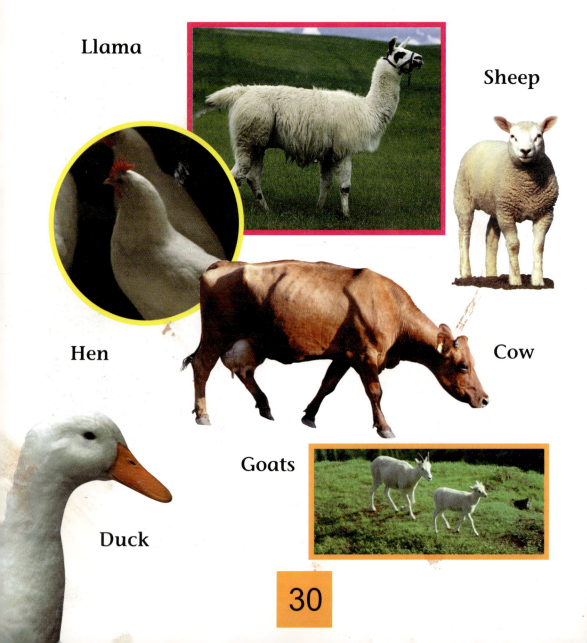

Llama

Sheep

Hen

Cow

Duck

Goats

Butter

Eggs

Wool jumper

Cheese

Milk

The answers are on page 32.

Index

Beak 28	Farmyard 3	Milking 15
Buffalo 26	Foot 29	
Bull 17		Pig 7
Butter 31	Goat 20, 30	Piglet 6
		Pulling a plough 26
Cattle 16	Hen 8, 30	
Cheese 31	Hoof 28	Sheep 19, 30
Chick 9	Horn 29	Sheepdog 23
Cockerel 8	Horse 24	Shepherd 22
Cow 14, 30		Snout 29
	Kid 12	
Duck 11, 30		
	Lamb 13	Tail 29
Eggs 31	Llama 27, 30	Turkey 10
Farm 5	Milk 31	Wool jumper 31

ANSWERS TO QUESTIONS

Page 28-29 – A chick has this **beak** • A goat has this **hoof** • A pig has this **snout** • A chick has this **foot** • A horse has this **tail** • A bull has these **horns**.

Pages 30-31 – We get **butter** from cows • We get **eggs** from hens and ducks • We get **wool** from sheep and llamas • We get **milk** and **cheese** from cows, sheep and goats.

Photocredits: Abbreviations: t-top, m-middle, b-bottom, r-right, l-left, centre. Cover, 2, 9, 10, 14, 28t, 28bl – Stockbyte. 1, 12, 17, 28m, 29b, 30mr, 30bl, 30br – John Foxx Images. 3, 11, 13, 31 all – Select Pictures. 4-5, 6, 8, 16, 18t, 18-19, 22, 26 both, 27, 30t, 30ml – Corbis Images. 15 – Christine Osborne/Corbis. 20-21, 23, 24-25, 29br, 30c – Digital Stock.
Illustrators: Wayne Ford – for Wildlife Art Ltd.